THE
THREE
BILLY GOATS
GRUFF

A FOLK TALE CLASSIC

Paul Galdone

For Kay

www.hmhbooks.com

The Library of Congress Cataloging-in-Publication data is on file.

ISBN: 978-0-395-28812-2 hardcover
ISBN: 978-0-89919-035-8 paperback
ISBN: 978-0-618-83685-7 big book
ISBN: 978-0-618-89499-4 book and CD
ISBN: 978-0-395-89899-4 book and cassette
ISBN: 978-0-547-57655-8 paper over board

Manufactured in China
LEO 10 9 8 7 6 5 4 3 2 1
4500292122

Houghton Mifflin Harcourt

Boston   New York

THE THREE BILLY GOATS GRUFF

Once upon a time there were three Billy Goats.
They lived in a valley and the name
of all three Billy Goats was "Gruff."

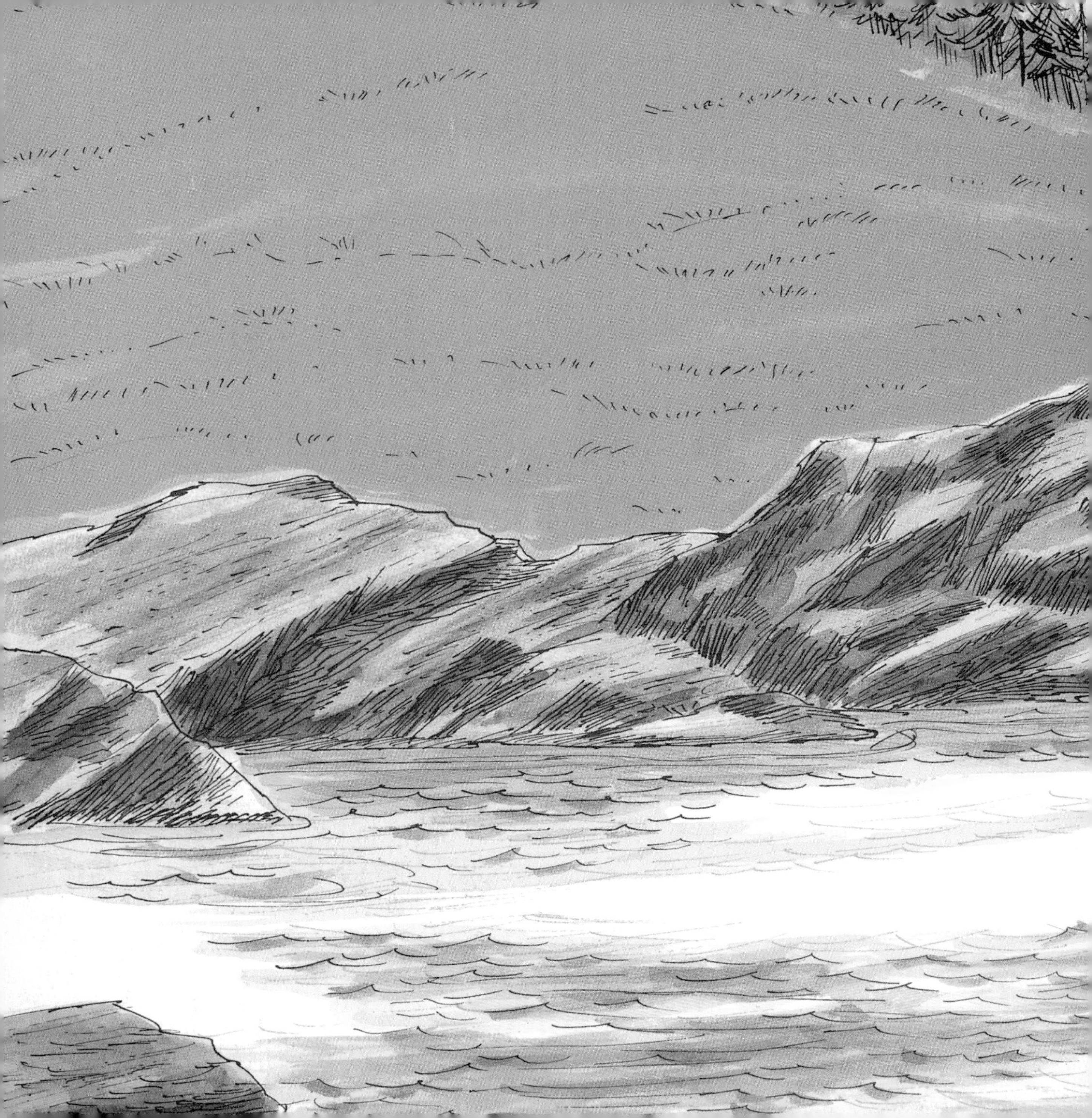

There was very little grass in the valley
and the Billy Goats were hungry.
They wanted to go up the hillside
to a fine meadow full of grass and daisies
where they could eat and eat and eat, and get fat.

But on the way up there was
a bridge over a rushing river.
And under the bridge lived a Troll
who was as mean as he was ugly.

First the youngest Billy Goat Gruff
decided to cross the bridge.

"TRIP, TRAP, TRIP, TRAP!" went the bridge.

"WHO'S THAT TRIPPING OVER MY BRIDGE?"
roared the Troll.

"Oh, it's only I, the tiniest Billy Goat Gruff,"
said the Billy Goat in his very small voice.
"And I'm going to the meadow to make myself fat."

"No you're not," said the Troll,
"for I'm coming to gobble you up!"

"Oh, please don't take me. I'm too little, that I am,"
said the Billy Goat. "Wait till the second
Billy Goat Gruff comes. He's much bigger."

"Well then, be off with you," said the Troll.

A little later the second Billy Goat Gruff came
to cross the bridge.

"TRIP, TRAP! TRIP, TRAP! TRIP, TRAP!"
went the bridge.

"WHO'S THAT TRIPPING OVER MY BRIDGE?"
roared the Troll.

"Oh, it's only I, the second Billy Goat Gruff,
and I'm going up to the meadow to make myself fat,
said the Billy Goat.
And his voice was not so small.

"No you're not," said the Troll,
"for I'm coming to gobble you up!"

"Oh, please don't take me. Wait a little, till the
third Billy Goat Gruff comes. He's much bigger."

"Very well, be off with you," said the Troll.

Then up came the third Billy Goat Gruff.

"TRIP, TRAP! TRIP, TRAP!
TRIP, TRAP! TRIP, TRAP!"
went the bridge.

The third Billy Goat Gruff was so heavy
that the bridge creaked and groaned under him.

"WHO'S THAT TRAMPING OVER MY BRIDGE?"
roared the Troll.

"IT IS I, THE BIG BILLY GOAT GRUFF,"
said the Billy Goat.
And his voice was as loud as the Troll's.

"Now I'm coming to gobble you up!" roared the Troll.

"Well, come along!" said the big Billy Goat Gruff.
"I've got two horns and four hard hooves.
See what you can do!"

So up climbed that mean, ugly Troll,
and the big Billy Goat Gruff butted him with his horns,
and he trampled him with his hard hooves,

and he tossed him over the bridge
into the rushing river.

Then the big Billy Goat Gruff went up the hillside
to join his brothers.

In the meadow
the three Billy Goats Gruff
got so fat that they could hardly
walk home again.
They are probably there yet.

So snip, snap, snout,
This tale's told out.